CW01660823

Trim

A Biographical Tribute to the Memory of

Trim

by Matthew Flinders

Illustrated by
Annette Macarthur-Onslow

Second edition for

Nauticalia

to celebrate
Matthew Flinders' circumnavigation and mapping of the coastline of Australia ... helped by Trim.
A lifelike model of Trim is one of the series of historic Intrepid Ships' Cats *designed by Nauticalia, Shepperton, England TW17 9LQ,*
Telephone: +44 (0) 1932 244 396
Fax: +44 (0) 1932 241 679
Internet: www.nauticalia.com
e-mail: shipscats@nauticalia.com

CORNSTALK PUBLISHING

To the memory of Trim,
the best and most illustrious of his Race,
the most affectionate of friends,
faithful of servants,
and best of creatures.
He made the Tour of the Globe,
and a voyage to Australia,
which he circumnavigated; and was ever the
delight and pleasure of his fellow voyagers.
Returning to Europe in 1803, he was shipwrecked
in the Great Equinoxial Ocean;
This danger escaped, he sought refuge and assistance
at the Isle of France, where
he was made prisoner, contrary to the laws of
Justice, of Humanity, and of French National Faith;

and where, alas! he terminated his useful
career, by an untimely death,
being devoured by the Catophagi of
that island.
Many a time have I beheld his little merriments
with delight,
and his superior intelligence with surprise:
Never will his like be seen again!
Trim was born in the Southern Indian Ocean,
in the Year 1799, and
perished as above at the Isle of France
in 1804.

Peace be to his shade, and
Honour to his memory

In this story Matthew Flinders changed the names of the ships on which he and Trim sailed:

Roundabout = *Reliance*

Spyall = *Investigator*

Janty = *Porpoise*

Minikin = *Cumberland*

(First name indicates Flinders's fictional title, the second the ship's real name.)

Preface

Matthew Flinders was only twenty-one when he arrived in Botany Bay in the year 1795. Indeed, Australia had only been settled by Europeans for seven years when he sailed through Sydney Heads. But Flinders was already a veteran of a naval battle at sea and of a trip to Tahiti with Captain William Bligh. In 1801 Flinders took charge of the *Investigator,* and in eighteen months circumnavigated the continent of Australia, mapping a large part of the unknown coastline. On his way back to England with the results of his work, Flinders was arrested by the French authorities on the island of Mauritius and detained there for seven agonising and frustrating years. He died in England, still a young man, in 1814.

Flinders was one of the greatest of explorers, and explorers like Cook and Robert O'Hara Burke and Robert Falcon Scott and, of course, Flinders himself, quickly become heroes to the rest of us. In the same way that they move out and away from civilisation, we lift them above common humanity and make myths and epics out of their lives. This is a pity in many ways, for immortality is really based on what people have in common, as every great novelist knows.

Sailors, in particular, keep themselves to themselves in their accounts of their great exploits, and they don't reveal much of their personalities to the world. That is why we are so lucky to have this little fun-piece by Matthew Flinders on his dearly loved cat Trim, whom he called "the best and most illustrious of his race". It shows Flinders as an affectionate, tolerant and humorous man. After reading this it would be hard to believe that he ran an unhappy ship. Indeed, perhaps this tells us as much as any other evidence does about some of the hidden reasons Flinders was able to achieve so much in so short a time.

The little essay has remained hidden in the archives of

the National Maritime Museum at Greenwich, England, for many years. Writers on Flinders have made little use of it, and it was only published for the first time in 1973, in the literary magazine *Overland*. I think it impossible for anyone to read this and still look upon Flinders as no more than a school-book hero.

Stephen Murray-Smith, 1977

Introduction

FLINDERS, Captain Matthew, R.N. (1774–1814), essayist ... None of the biographical dictionaries begin their entry *that* way. Matthew Flinders is not remembered as a literary man. His fame lies in his explorations, his skill as a navigator, his innovations in hydrographic cartography and his experiments on magnetism in ships (no one before had noted that the cannon and other ironware in ships affected the binnacle compass). He was depicted, in sepia-toned steel engravings on the margarine-and-mustard coloured walls of countless primary-school rooms, as chief barber to the Aboriginals on the shores of Lake Illawarra.

The late K.A. Austin published an article on Flinders's writings[1], but Flinders has rarely been styled "author", let alone "essayist" and he would probably be the last to claim either title for himself. His "Biographical Tribute to Trim the Cat" is, however, in the tradition of the eighteenth-century English essay and its style owes much to Laurence Sterne's *Tristram Shandy*, whence came Trim's name.

In the novel Tristram tells us that his uncle's servant, James Butler, went by the name of Trim, "and of excellent use was he, attending my uncle Toby … with great fidelity and affection."

While preparations for the departure of the *Investigator* were under way in 1801, Flinders had reservations about his ability to write the account of the voyage that would be required of him, and had already discussed the possibility of help from literary friends. Publication of his *Observations on the Coasts of Van Dieman's Land* (1801) left him sure that "authorship sits awkwardly upon me", but already his pen was busy and becoming a familiar tool. A steady stream of letters went ashore from the *Investigator* to Sir Joseph Banks, the Lords of Admiralty and the Navy Board, seeking to hasten the departure of the ship. During the voyage comprehensive and detailed observations of all the places visited swelled his Journal, and from Sydney reports of the voyage's progress and disasters went to Sir Joseph Banks and Their Lordships. During his imprisonment in Mauritius from 1803 to 1809, authorship, sitting less awkwardly, became even more familiar. He was busy writing: writing letters and reports of his imprisonment to everyone who might be able to obtain his release; writing an edited fair copy of his Journal for presentation to the Admiralty; writing the first of his papers on magnetism in ships; writing a memoir on the construction of his charts, and his methods of establishing latitude and longitude and variation of the compass; writing a manual on spherical trigonometry and navigation; and, late in his imprisonment, the "Tribute to Trim".

"This contrived little essay", however one evaluates its literary merit (remembering that it was written in an age of verbosity), is of interest for two reasons: for the light it throws on early-nineteenth century shipboard life, and especially for its revelation of its author. It shows the same keen observation, here of cats and men, that is seen in the careful description of places in the *Voyage to Terra Australis*. It shows his sense of fun and humour, and above all the warmth of his affection, not only for Trim, but for men, that is to be seen in his care for his crew, the close touch that he kept with many of them after his return to England, and the maintenance of friendships with former shipmates long after personal contact had been severed for years. He must have been an amiable and likable man and a congenial companion.

Among his friends, Trim held a special place. Trim joined Flinders soon after he had taken his lieutenant's examination in Cape Town while the *Reliance* was there getting supplies for hungry Sydney. Trim shared the voyage to Moreton Bay in the *Norfolk*, and to England in the *Reliance*; the excitement of preparing for the *Investigator*'s voyage, and the joys of Flinders's early married life before the ship left England. He circumnavigated Australia and, like the rest of the ship's company, endured malnutrition and illness off the Arnhem Land coast. In June 1803 Flinders wrote to his wife from Sydney: "Trim, like his master, is becoming grey: he is at present fat and frisky, and takes meat from our forks with his usual dexterity: he is commonly my bedfellow." Trim survived the foundering of the *Porpoise* and, after six weeks on Wreck Reef, rejoined his master on the *Cumberland* to go to England but to be detained at Mauritius. He was Flinders's constant companion in the period of Flinders's greatest achievements, and his loss, coming soon after most of the ship's company had been repatriated, was at a time when Flinders's fortunes seemed to have reached their lowest ebb.

Besides writing, Flinders had other interests on Mauritius. He was reading widely in both French and English, he was teaching a group of children mathematics, had an interest in a plantation (that was not particularly successful) and played the flute (he took it to be repaired soon after arriving in London). At times anger, frustration, and illness plagued him, but there was also a resignation to, and acceptance of, his situation: he was imprisoned but none the less interested and busy. It is as evidence that, despite imprisonment, the human qualities of the man endured that the "Tribute to Trim" is important.

James D. Mack finds it "uncharacteristic of Flinders's other writings" and comments that it shows "an unmistakable boyish warmth in the man, a warmth that comes as a pleasant surprise at this stage of Flinders's life".[2] It is uncharacteristic in so far that his other writings were official and scientific. They were respectful and decorously worded letters and reports to his superiors and patrons: not places for wit, or fancy (though they do contain occasional glimpses of impishness – the naming of Antechamber Bay, The Pages and Backstairs Passage; and the naming in honour of Admiral Troubridge, who ran aground during the Battle of the Nile, of the largest shoal in Spencers Gulf). It is uncharacteristic in so far as it is a parody of some of the more ponderous "learned" works of the time, but its wit is not uncharacteristic of his private letters and diaries: "My appetite is so good that I believe it has the intention of revenging me on the Governor by occasioning a famine in the land." The "Tribute", a *jeu d'esprit,* may be surprising after six years' detention, but it is sure proof that while Decaen and Mauritius held the man, the mind and the spirit were unconfined, and that even after five years the heart still mourned "the most affectionate of friends, faithful of servants, and best of creatures".

T.M. Perry

Footnotes:

1. K.A. Austin, "Matthew Flinders as an Author", *Proceedings of the Royal Geographical Society of Australasia, South Australian Branch,* Vol. 67 (1966), pp. 39–46
2. James, D. Mack, *Matthew Flinders 1774–1814* (Melbourne, Nelson, 1966), pp. 209–210

I can never speak of cats without a sentiment of regret for my poor Trim, the favourite of all our ship's company on the *Spyall*. This good-natured purring animal was born on board His Majesty's ship the *Roundabout* in 1799 during a passage from the Cape of Good Hope to Botany Bay; and saving the rights and titles of the Parish of Stepney, was consequently an Indian by birth. The signs of superior intelligence which marked his infancy procured for him an education beyond what is usually bestowed upon the individuals of his tribe; and being brought up amongst sailors, his manner acquired a peculiarity of cast which rendered them as different from those of other cats as the actions of a fearless seaman are from those of a lounging, shame-faced ploughboy. It was, however, from his gentleness and the innate goodness of his heart that I gave him the name of my uncle Toby's honest, kind-hearted, humble companion.

In playing with his little brothers and sisters upon deck by moonlight, when the ship was lying tranquilly in harbour, the energy and elasticity of his movements sometimes carried him so far beyond his mark that he fell overboard; but this was

far from being a misfortune; he learned to swim and to have no dread of water; and when a rope was thrown over to him, he took hold of it like a man, and ran up it like a cat. In a short time he was able to mount up the gangway steps quicker than his master, or even than the first lieutenant.

Being a favourite with everybody on board, both officers and seamen, he was well fed, and grew fast both in size and comeliness. A description of his person will not be misplaced here. From the care that was taken of him, and the force of his own constitution, Trim grew to be one of the finest animals I ever saw. His size emulated that of his friends of Angora: his weight being from ten to

twelve pounds, according as our *fresh-meatometer* stood high or low. His tail was long, large, and bushy; and when he was animated by the presence of a stranger of the anti-catean race, it bristled out to a fearful size, whilst vivid flashes darted from his fiery eyes, though at other times he was candour and good nature itself. His head was small and round – his physiognomy bespoke intelligence and confidence – his whiskers were long and graceful, and his ears were cropped in a beautiful curve. Trim's robe was a clear jet black, with the exception of his four feet, which seemed to have been dipped in snow, and his underlip, which rivalled them in whiteness. He had also a white star on his breast, and it seemed as if nature had designed him for the prince and model of his race: I doubt whether Whittington's cat, of which so much has been said and written, was to be compared to him.

Notwithstanding my great partiality to my friend Trim, strict justice obliges me to cite in this place a trait in his character which by many will be thought a blemish: he was, I am sorry to say it, excessively vain of his person, particularly of his snow-white feet. He would frequently place himself on the quarterdeck before the officers, in the middle of their walk; and spreading out his two white hands in the posture of the *lion couchant*,

oblige them to stop and admire him. They would indeed say low to each other, "See the vanity of that cat!" but they could not help admiring his graceful form and beautiful white feet. Indeed, when it is known that to the finest form ever beheld he joined extraordinary personal and mental qualifications, the impossibility that the officers could be angry with him must be evident; and they were men of too much elevation of mind to be jealous of him. I would not be an advocate in the cause of vanity; but if it is ever excusable, it was so in this case. How many men are there, who have no claim either from birth, fortune, or acquirements, personal or mental, whose vanity is not to be confined within such harmless bounds, as was that of Trim! And I will say for him that he never spoke ill of or objected to the pretensions of others, which is more than can be said for very many bipeds.

Trim, though vain as we have seen, was not like those young men who, being assured of an independence, spend their youth in idle trifling, and consider all serious application as pedantic and derogatory, or at least to be useless; he was, on the contrary, animated with a noble zeal for the improvement of his faculties. His exercises commenced with acquiring the art of leaping over the hands; and as every man in the ship took pleasure in instructing him, he at length arrived to such a pitch of perfection that I am persuaded, had nature placed him in the empire of Lilliput, his merit would have promoted him to the first offices in the state.

He was taught to lie flat upon the deck on his back, with his four feet stretched out like one dead; and in this posture he would remain until a signal was given him to rise, whilst his preceptor resumed his walk backwards and forwards; if, however, he was kept in this position, which it must be confessed was not very agreeable to a quadruped, a slight motion of the end of his tail denoted the commencement of impatience, and his friends never pushed their lesson further.

Trim took a fancy to learning the art of nautical astronomy. When an officer took lunar or other observations, he would place himself by the

timekeeper and consider the motion of the hands, and apparently the uses of the instrument, with much earnest attention. He would try to touch the second hand, listen to the ticking, and walk all round the piece to assure himself whether or no it might be a living animal; and mewing to the young gentleman whose business it was to mark down the

time, seemed to ask an explanation. When the officer had made his observation, the cry of "Stop!" roused Trim from his meditations; he cocked his tail and, running up the rigging near to the officer, mewed at him to know the meaning of all those proceedings.

Finding at length that nature had not designed him for an astronomer, Trim had too much good sense to continue a useless pursuit; but a musket ball slung with a piece of twine, and made to whirl round upon the deck by a slight motion of the finger, never failed to attract his notice and to give him pleasure; perhaps from bearing a near resemblance to the movement of his favourite planet the moon, in her orbit round the primary which we inhabit. He was equally fond of making experiments upon projectile forces and the power of gravity. If a ball was thrown gently along the deck, he would pursue it; and when the gravitating principle combined with the friction overcame the impelling power, he would give the ball a fresh impetus, but generally to turn its direction into an elliptic curve (at other times the form of the earth appeared to be the object of his experiments, and his ball was made to describe an oblate spheroid). The seamen took advantage of this his propensity to making experiments with globular bodies; and two of them would often place themselves, one at each end of the forecastle, and trundling a ball backwards and forwards from one to the other, would keep Trim in constant action running after it; his admiration of the planetary system having induced an habitual passion for everything round that was in motion. Could Trim have had the benefit of an Orrery, or of being present at Mr Walker's experiments in natural philosophy, there can be no doubt as to the progress he would have made in the sublimest of sciences.

His desire to gain a competent knowledge in practical seamanship was not less than he showed for experimental philosophy. The replacing of a topmast carried away, or taking a reef in the sails, were what most attracted his attention at sea; and at all times, when there was more bustle upon deck than usual, he never failed to be present and in the midst of it; for as I have before hinted, he was endowed with an unusual degree of confidence and courage, and having never received anything but good from men, he believed all to be his friends, and he was the friend of all. When the nature of the bustle upon deck was not understood by him, he would mew and rub his back up against the legs of one and the other, frequently at the risk of being trampled underfoot, until he obtained the attention of someone to satisfy him. He knew what

good discipline required, and on taking in a reef, never presumed to go aloft until the order was issued; but so soon as the officer had given the words "Away up aloft!", up he jumped along with the seamen; and so active and zealous was he that none could reach the top before or so soon as he did. His zeal, however, never carried him beyond a sense of dignity: he did not lay out on the yard like a common seaman, but always remained seated upon the cap, to inspect like an officer. This assumption of authority to which, it must be confessed, his rank, though great as a quadruped, did not entitle him amongst men, created no jealousy; for he always found some good friend ready to caress him after the business was done, and to take him down in his arms.

In harbour, the measuring of log and lead lines upon deck, and the stowage of the holds below, were the favourite subjects of his attention. No sooner was a cask moved than he darted in under it upon the enemies of his king and country, at the imminent risk of having his head crushed to atoms, which he several times very narrowly escaped. In the bread room he was still more indefatigable; he frequently solicited to be left there alone and in the dark, for two or three days together, that nothing might interrupt him in the discharge of his duty. This was one of the brightest traits in my friend Trim's character, and would indeed do honour to any character. In making the following deductions from it I shall not, I think, be accused of an unjust partiality. First, it must be evident that he had no fear of evil spirits, and consequently that he had a conscience above

reproach. Second, it is clear that he possessed a degree of patience and perseverance of which few men can boast; and third, that like a faithful subject he employed all these estimable qualities in the service of His Majesty's faithful servants, and indirectly of His Majesty himself. Alas! my poor Trim, thy extraordinary merit required only to be known, in order to excite universal admiration.

Trim was admitted upon the table of almost every officer and man in the ship: in the gunroom he was always the first ready for dinner, but though he was commonly seated a quarter of an hour before any other person, his modest reserve was such that his voice was not heard until everybody else was served. He then put in his request, not for a full allowance – he was too modest – nor did he desire there should be laid for him a plate, knife, fork or spoon, with all which he could very well dispense, but by a gentle caressing mew he petitioned for a little, little bit, a kind of tythe from the plate of each; and it was to no purpose to refuse it, for Trim was enterprising in time of need, as he was gentle and well bred in ordinary times. Without the greatest attention to each morsel, in the person whom he had petitioned in vain, he would whip it off the fork with his paw, on its passage to the mouth, with such dexterity and an air so graceful that it rather excited admiration than anger. He did not, however, leap off the table with his prize, as if he had done wrong; but putting the morsel into his mouth and eating it quietly, would go to the next person and repeat his little *mew*; if refused his wonted tythe, he stood ready to take all advantages. There are some men so inconsiderate as to be talking when they should be eating, who keep their meat suspended in mid-air till a semi-colon in the discourse gives an opportunity of taking their mouthful without interrupting their story. Guests of this description were a dead mark for Trim: when a short pause left them time to take the prepared mouthful, they were often surprised to find their meat gone, they could not tell how.

Trim had one day missed a fine morsel from the hungry activity of one of the young gentlemen who dined in the gunroom. Seeing him, however, talking and eating at the same time, my persevering gentleman did not give it up, though the piece was half masticated and only waited for a period to disappear; but running up the waistcoat of our unsuspecting guest, for Trim was then but a kitten, and placing one paw at each corner of his mouth, he laid vigorous siege to his morsel; and whilst the astonished midshipman inarticulately exclaimed, "G_d d_ _n the cat!" Trim fairly took the piece out of his mouth and carried it off. This was pushing his enterprises too far, and he therefore received a reprimand which prevented them in future.

The gunroom steward was, however, more particularly Trim's confidant; and though he had dined with the masters, he was not too proud to sit

down a second time with the servant. William had such an opinion of Trim's intelligence that he talked to him as to his child, whilst my four-footed master, looking up in his face, seemed to understand him and to give rational answers. They had the following conversation after dinner on the day of Trim's audacious enterprise just related:

"Do you know, master Trim, that you have behaved very ill?" – Me-ew?

"It is very well to play your tricks with them that know you, but you should be more modest with strangers." – Mew!

"How dare you say that I gave you no breakfast?

Did I not give you all the milk that was left, and some bread soaked in it?" – Mou-wow!

"No meat! What! you grow insolent? I'll chain you up; do you hear, Sir!" – Me-ew.

"Well, if you'll promise to behave better, you shall have a nice piece off the cold shank of mutton for your supper, you shall." – Mew-wew!

"Gently, master Trim. I'll give it you now, but first promise me upon your honour." – We-wee.

"Come then, my good boy, come up and kiss me."

Trim leaped up on his shoulder and, rubbing his face against William's cheek, received the mutton piece by piece out of his mouth.

In an expedition made to examine the northern parts of the coast of New South Wales, Trim presented a request to be of the party, promising to take upon himself the defence of our bread bags, and his services were accepted. Bongaree, an intelligent native of Port Jackson, was also on

board our little sloop; and with him Trim formed an intimate acquaintance. If he had occasion to drink, he mewed to Bongaree and leaped up to the water cask; if to eat, he called him down below and went straight to his kid, where there was generally a remnant of black swan. In short, Bongaree was his great resource, and his kindness was repaid with caresses. In times of danger, Trim never showed any signs of fear; and it may truly be said that he never distrusted or was afraid of any man.

In 1800, the *Roundabout* returned to England by the way of Cape Horn and St Helena; and thus Trim, besides his other voyages, completed the tour of the globe. Many and curious are the observations which he made in various branches of science, particularly in the natural history of small quadrupeds, birds and flying fish, for which he had much taste. These, with his remarks upon man and manners, if future leisure should enable me to put into order, I may perhaps give to the world; and from the various seas and countries he has visited, joined to his superior powers for distinguishing obscure subjects, and talents for seizing them, these observations may be expected to be more interesting than the imaginary adventures of your guineas, shillings or half-pence, and to possess more originality than the Turkish spy.

Trim was not only a stranger to England, but also to a house and to the manner of living in it: the king of Bantam's ambassador was not more inexperienced in these matters than he. I took a lodging for him at Deptford, placing him under the guardianship of the good woman of the house, who promised to instruct him in the usages of terra firma; but she knew not what she had undertaken. He would go out at the sash window to the top of the house, for the convenience of making his observations on the surrounding country more at ease. If it came on to rain, the sash was put down. This would have been an invincible obstacle to other cats, but not so to Trim: he bolted through the glass like a clap of thunder, to the great alarm of the good hostess below. "Good Gad, Trim," exclaimed she on entering the chamber, "is it thee? They said thou wast a strange outlandish cat, and verily I think thou art the divil: I must shut thee up, for if thou go'st to treat neighbours thus, I shall have thee taken up for a burglary; but come, I know thy master will pay the damage: has thou cut thyself?"

Woe to the good woman's china if Trim got into her closet. Your delicate town-bred cats go mincing in amongst cups and saucers without touching them; but Trim! If he spied a mouse there he dashed at it like a man of war, through thick and thin: the splinters flew in all directions. The poor woman at first thought an evil spirit was playing pranks in her cupboard – she opens the door with fear and trembling when, to her infinite dismay, out jumps my black gentleman upon her shoulder: she was well nigh dead with fear. Seeing how much mischief was done to her dear china, the pride of her heart, she seized Trim to beat him soundly; but instead of trying to escape, the droll

animal rubs his whiskers up against her chin and falls to purring. She had no longer the heart to strike him; but after a moment's hesitation, she heaved a sigh and picked up the pieces.

I took him up to London in the stage coach, and as there were no fine ladies to be frightened at the presence of a strange cat, he was left at full liberty. He was not in the least disconcerted by the novelty of his situation; but placing himself upon the seat, and stretching out his white paws, conducted himself reasonably like any other passenger; to the admiration of two gentlemen who did not cease to make inquiries concerning his education, manners, and adventures, during the whole way to town.

A worthy acquaintance in London took Trim into his family; but he soon requested me to take him back, for "such a strange animal," said he, "I never saw. I am afraid of losing him. He goes out into the streets in the middle of the day, and rubs himself against the legs of people passing by. Several have taken him up to caress him, but I fear someone will be carrying him off."

I took him on board the *Spyall* to make a second voyage to the South Seas. Trim now found himself at home; and his gentleness and extraordinary confidence, joined to the amusement his droll antics furnished them, soon made him as great a favourite with his new shipmates as he had been on board the *Roundabout*.

We had several dogs on board the *Spyall*, but Trim was undisputed master of them all. When they were at play upon the deck, he would go in amongst them with his stately air; and giving a blow at the eyes of one, and a scratch on the nose to another, oblige them to stand out of his way. He was capable

of being animated against a dog, as dogs usually may be against a cat; and I have more than once sent him from the quarter-deck to drive a dog off the forecastle. He would run half the way briskly, crouching like a lion which has prey in view; but then, assuming a majestic deportment, and without being deterred by the menacing attitude of his opponent, he would march straight up to him and

give him a blow on the nose, accompanied with a threatening *mew!* If the dog did not immediately retreat, Trim flew at him with his war cry of *Yow!* If resistance was still made, he leaped up on the rail over his head and so bespattered him about the eyes that he was glad to run off howling. Trim pursued him till he took refuge below; and then returned smiling to his master to receive his caresses.

During our circumnavigation of Australia in the years 1801, 1802 and 1803, Trim had frequent opportunities of repeating his observations and experiments in his favourite science, natural history, and of exerting his undiminished

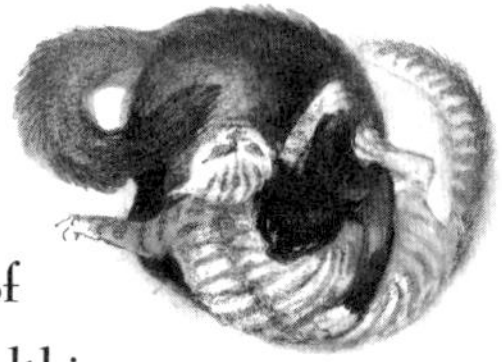

activity and zeal for the public good. In the Gulf of Carpentaria, from the unhealthiness of the climate, the want of his usual fresh food, and perhaps from too much application to study, this worthy creature became almost grey, lost much of weight, and seemed to be threatened with a premature old age; but to the great joy of his friends, he re-assumed his fine black robe and his accustomed portliness, a short time after returning to harbour.

Only once was Trim known to be guilty of theft: he had a soul above it; but one unlucky afternoon a cold leg of mutton in the pantry tempted him.

Being unable to carry it off himself, he got the assistance of Van, a Dutch cat on board; and they had so far succeeded as to get it down off the shelf, and were dragging it together into the hold, when lo! the steward came and surprised them in the fact. Van made his escape, but Trim, ever confident, made no efforts, and was seized and beaten soundly. He took the blows with philosophical patience; but no sooner was he set at liberty than he ran after his false Dutch friend, and repaid him with interest the beating he had received. The recital of this unfortunate anecdote of my friend Trim will, I hope, be received as a proof of the impartiality of the history; and I advertise the reader not to seek in it for any political allegory, but to be assured that the facts were really such as they are here related.

The *Spyall* being found to be rotten, Trim embarked on board His Majesty's ship the *Janty* to return to England, and was shipwrecked with us upon a coral bank in the Great Equinoxial Ocean on the night of August 17, 1803. The imagination can scarcely attain to what Trim had to suffer during this dreadful night, but his courage was not beaten down. He got to Wreck Reef Bank with the crew, and passed there two long and dreary months, during which his zeal in the provision tent was not less than it had been in the bread room, and his manners preserved all their amiability. When vessels arrived to our assistance, Trim preferred following his master on board the *Minikin* schooner to going with the rest of the ship's company to China in a large

vessel, giving thereby a memorable example of faithful attachment.

The *Minikin*, being very leaky, was obliged to stop at the Isle of France; and there poor Trim, his master and few followers were all made prisoners, under the pretext that they had come to spy out the nakedness of the land, though it was clear as day that they knew nothing of the war that had taken place a few months before. Trim was confined in a room with his master and another officer; and as he possessed more philosophy than we did, he contributed by his gay humour to soften our straight captivity; but sometimes also he contrived to elude the vigilance of the sentinel at the door, and left us to make little temporary excursions in the neighbourhood. It is probable that he made some new secret acquaintances in these visits, for they became more frequent than was prudent; and for fear of accidents, we were obliged to shut him up after supper.

On our being removed to the Maison Despeaux amongst the prisoners of war, a French lady offered to be Trim's security, in order to have him for a companion to her little daughter; and the fear of some clandestine proceedings on the part of the soldiers of the guard induced me to comply, on finding it would give no umbrage to His Excellency the French governor and captain-general. A fortnight had scarcely passed when the public gazette of the island announced that Trim was nowhere to be found, and offered a reward of ten Spanish dollars to anyone who would conduct him back to his afflicted little mistress. My sorrow may be better conceived than described; I would with pleasure have given fifty dollars to have had my friend and companion restored to me. All research and offers of recompense were in vain, poor Trim was effectually lost; and it is but too probable that this excellent unsuspecting animal was stewed and eaten by some hungry black slave, in whose eyes all his merits could not balance against the avidity excited by his sleek body and fine furred skin.

Thus perished my faithful intelligent Trim! The sporting, affectionate and useful companion of my voyages during four years. Never, my Trim, "to take thee all in all, shall I see thy like again"; but never wilt thou cease to be regretted by all who had the pleasure of knowing thee. And for thy affectionate master and friend, he promises thee, if ever he shall have the happiness to enjoy repose in his native country, under a thatched cottage surrounded by half an acre of land, to erect in the most retired corner a monument to perpetuate thy memory and record thy uncommon merits.

The author

Matthew Flinders was born in England in 1774. He joined the navy in 1790 and spent the years 1795 to 1799 charting Australian waters. Then, in 1801, Flinders circumnavigated Australia aboard the *Investigator*. On his way back to England he was detained on Mauritius for seven years by the French. It was during this period that Flinders wrote his story about Trim.

The illustrator

Annette Macarthur-Onslow began her career as puppeteer and commercial artist in her homeland, Australia, then worked as a freelance illustrator in England and France, and as a production assistant to a London publisher. Her own books include *Uhu*, *Minie* and *The Round House* (inspired by years in a Cotswold cottage). Her Australian work includes a full-colour picture book, *The Man from Snowy River*.

State Library of NSW information

On 28 March 1996, Rear-Admiral David Campbell, A.M., R.A.N., unveiled a bronze statue to Captain Matthew Flinders's cat, Trim. The ceremony took place in the presence of the State Librarian, Dagmar Schmidmaier, along with some four hundred guests, donors and well-wishers, and was accompanied by the Naval Reserve Band.

The bronze statue of Trim was sculpted by John Cornwell and stands on the windowsill of the Mitchell Library on Macquarie Street, just behind the tall figure of his master. A nearby plaque commemorates the first circumnavigation of Australia by Captain Flinders from 1801 to 1803.

The Library Shop (State Library of NSW, Macquarie St, Sydney) has developed a range of Trim merchandise, including bronze replicas of the statue, key rings, brooches, T-shirts, polo shirts and caps.

Visitors to the statue can now enjoy light refreshments in a garden setting at Café Trim, located at the base of Trim's master's statue.

Angus&Robertson
An imprint of HarperCollins*Publishers*

First published in *Overland* No. 55, 1973
Children's edition published in 1977 by William Collins Publishers Pty Limited
Reprinted in 1978
This Cornstalk edition published in 2005 by HarperCollins*Publishers*
ACN 009 913 517
A member of the HarperCollins*Publishers* (Australia) Pty Limited Group

Text copyright © Lisette Flinders Petrie 1973
Illustrations copyright © Annette Macarthur-Onslow 1985

This book is copyright.
Apart from any fair dealing for the purposes of private study, research, criticism or review, as permitted under the Copyright Act, no part may be reproduced by any process without written permission.
Inquiries should be addressed to the publishers.

HarperCollins*Publishers*
25 Ryde Road, Pymble, Sydney, NSW 2073, Australia
31 View Road, Glenfield, Auckland 10, New Zealand
77–85 Fulham Palace Road, London W6 8JB, United Kingdom
Hazelton Lanes, 55 Avenue Road, Suite 2900, Toronto, Ontario M5R 3L2
and 1995 Markham Road, Scarborough, Ontario M1B 5M8, Canada
10 East 53rd Street, New York NY 10032, USA

National Library of Australia Cataloguing-in-Publication data:

Flinders, Matthew, 1774–1814
Trim
ISBN 0 732 28284 5.
1. Flinders, Matthew, 1774–1814 – Juvenile literature. 2. Trim (Cat).
3. Cats – Juvenile literature. I. Macarthur-Onslow, Annette. II Title.
A828.103

Printed in China

9 8 7 6 5 4 3 2 1